KU-453-014

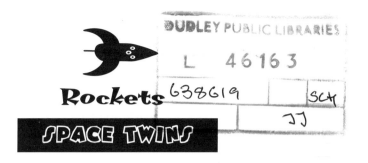

Rockets

SPACE TWINS

Time Travellers

Wendy Smith

A & C Black • London

Rockets series:

CROOK CATCHERS - Karen Wallace & Judy Brown

HAUNTED MOUSE - Dee Shulman

LITTLE T - Frank Rodgers

MOTLEY'S CREW - Margaret Ryan &
Margaret Chamberlain

MR CROC - Frank Rodgers

MRS MAGIC - Wendy Smith

MY FUNNY FAMILY - Colin West

ROVER - Chris Powling & Scoular Anderson

SILLY SAUSAGE - Michaela Morgan & Dee Shulman

SPACE TWINS - Wendy Smith

WIZARD'S BOY - Scoular Anderson

Published 2002 by A & C Black Publishers Ltd
37 Soho Square, London W1D 3QZ
www.acblack.com

Text and illustrations copyright © 2002 Wendy Smith

The right of Wendy Smith to be identified as author
and illustrator of this work has been asserted by her
in accordance with the Copyright, Designs and Patents Act 1988.

ISBN 0-7136-6111-9

A CIP catalogue record for this book is available
from the British Library.

A & C Black uses paper produced with elemental
chlorine-free pulp, harvested from managed sustainable forests.

Printed and bound by G. Z. Printek, Bilbao, Spain.

Chapter One

Far, far away, beyond our dimension of time, flies the good ship Zazaza.

Each night it sends a signal.

Zooming in through the clear sky, we can see the source.

Before they go to sleep, Mik and Mak, the space twins, beam their message.

Here on Earth, in East Volesey*,
Wilbur and his Space Spotter Squad
are listening keenly.

*a suburb on the fringe of nowhere.

At that moment, Zuna the Dream Supervisor entered the Galactaglobe and cut the signal.

Wilbur was disappointed.

However, not everyone at St Volesey's was as thrilled when the headmistress welcomed their special guest.

The Professor did his best to explain the wonders of the Universe.

The Professor went on...

...and on...

Alas, neither did the pupils of St Volesey's.

The headmistress thanked the Professor.

There was an embarrassing silence until...

...but nobody wanted to ask a single question.

Chapter Two

Wilbur and the squad watched sadly as the Professor drove home.

That very night, Wilbur and his Space Spotter Squad spoke with Mik and Mak again.

Mik and Mak thought they could help,
but how? They asked Zuna.

Zuna wasn't sure either.

But Captain Lupo was flattered to be asked.

He turned up the Wundascope to
examine planetary conditions.

One more time Zuna, Mik and Mak
urged the Captain to help them.

After some humming and haa-ing
he made his decision.

Chapter Three

Captain Lupo's instructions were beamed to Earth.

Tanglemere Common was near enough.
Getting the Professor there could be
tricky.

In the end, they decided to deliver an anonymous note.

The message read:

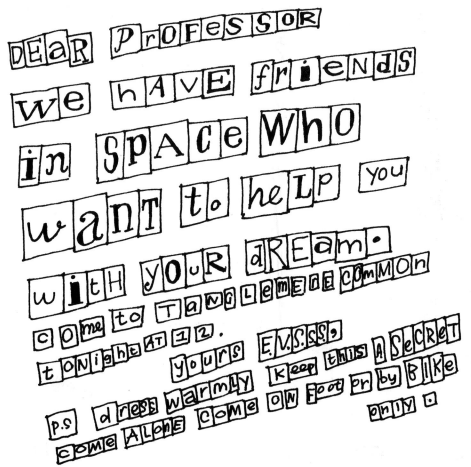

The Professor was puzzled.

That night, Wilbur and the squad were careful to be on their best behaviour.

Later they crept out into the night and cycled to Tanglemere Common.

They lay in wait for Professor Parrott.

Just as the Professor arrived,
a great orb of light beamed
down, whisking him into
the Teletransporter.

strange humming

hot light

phew!

To their surprise Wilbur, Ted and
Ziggy went up too.

Chapter Four

And that is how the Professor, Wilbur and his Space Spotter Squad found themselves aboard the Zazaza.

It was a relief when Captain Lupo
undid the Teletransporter hatch.

Mik and Mak proudly gave their friends a tour of the ship.

29

The Professor wrote pages of notes.

Captain Lupo was eager to show the
Professor his Spacelab.

The Professor was, well, over the moon.

And so was Zuna.

All too soon it was time to return to Earth.

Chapter Five

Coming back in the Teletransporter was a historical experience in every sense.

millions of light years
Was that a Beatle, just then?
I don't think so, dear boy.
a yokel

In a trice they landed on Tanglemere
Common. Everything was more or less
as they had left it.

As the Teletransporter spun forward into time, they rode home as fast as they could.

But Wilbur's parents had only been worried by the fact that he had gone to bed so early.

Ziggy's mum was up half the night with a sick hamster. She didn't notice a thing.

Ted's mum and dad had gone out, leaving Granny in charge.

Back at home, the Professor had only one thing on his mind. He was going to write a book about about his trip in space.

So, everything carried on as normal. Although Wilbur's mum wasn't quite sure all was entirely well.

Chapter Six

All in all, the abduction was a major success. But it was annoying having to keep it a secret.

Wilbur's mum worried about his ears,
until Zuna beamed down some stardust.

Wilbur and his friends barely mentioned
their trip to space. Except to Mik and
Mak.

The Professor's book was an
instant bestseller.

He used some of
Wilbur's snaps,
which showed
an interesting
time-lapse.

LOOK

07. 05. 20000002

Now, he was invited all over
the world.

He was hailed wherever he went.

In East Volesey, he became a huge local celebrity overnight.

Of course he never revealed the secret of his success.

And so the Professor remembered both his friends on Earth and his friends in space...

...who each night send a signal.